The Man Without a Planet

The Man Without a Planet

David Gerrold

Star Traveler Press

FIRST TRADE PAPERBACK EDITION

The Man Without a Planet

Copyright © 2025 by David Gerrold

Printed in the United States of America and internationally

This is a work of fiction. Names, character, places, and incidents, either are the product of the author's imagination or are used fictitiously. Any resemblance to actual persons, living or dead, events or locales is entirely coincidental.

Editor and Publisher, Justin T. O'Conor Sloane
Cover art: *Falling* © 2025 by Bob Eggleton
Interior book design by Erin Stocco of Modern Book Design

ISBN-13: 979-8-9925058-1-8 (Paperback)
ISBN-13: 979-8-9925058-2-5 (eBook)

Published by Star Traveler Press
An Imprint of Starship Sloane Publishing Company, Inc.
Austin-Round Rock, Texas
starshipsloane.com

Table of Contents

Editor's Note

Dear Reader,

Thanks for being here. I am confident that you will greatly enjoy reading this, David's newest novella, *The Man Without a Planet*. As a fan of the earthbound classic, *The Man Without a Country*, I sat up quick and straight in my chair when David mentioned in an email that he was working on this book. This svelte novella is a brilliant reimagining of the original and destined, I hope, for a spot in the literary canon and not just that of science fiction. It is the ideal companion piece to the first and is a narrative evolution that seems, in retrospect, to have been a grand inevitability. Elegantly crafted, this story is a starship propelled by hard-science-fiction engines that will take you into deep space and likewise, deep into the mind of our belligerent antihero Redmonde, whose worldview, social skills and temperament leave as much to be desired as the eternal state of exile in which he regrettably finds himself. I mentioned to David that although I agreed that Redmonde is indeed obnoxious, he nonetheless possesses a certain tenacity of perspective and a resolute clarity that is refreshing. I kind of liked the character actually, perhaps due to my own contrarian streak—but unquestionably because of the writing. Anyway, no wishy-washiness and no contrition, feigned or otherwise, with our hard-to-like friend, Redmonde. He sticks to his guns and he perseveres. His isolation and confinement serving only to fully cure the cement of his thinking, and in that, no cracks appear.

Unlike some of the antiheroes that immediately come to mind, like those played to great effect by Clint Eastwood, Redmonde does very little, if anything, of redeeming value—but for his final and unintentional contribution to the betterment of humanity. From the high society lounges of the glitterships to a windowless room tucked away in the crew's quarters, Redmonde's life, in its abrupt descent from a rarified, chattering privilege to the nearly monkish conditions of his soft imprisonment and the challenges of a sanctioned isolation that is less literal than strictly regulated, becomes an exploration of the consequences of philosophical inflexibility and the formative experiences of one's youth. Ah, the poor fellow? No, not really. In this story, David intertwines searing social commentary—of which he is a master weaponeer—with a holistic examination of the players and politics involved.

The best literature connects us boldly to the world around us and to the events that transpire therein, making us contemplate many things, sometimes reluctantly. I cannot help but think that if the technologies described in this novella currently existed, many of us would find ourselves, like Redmonde, in a permanent deep space exile.

I read this magnificent story in one intoxicating gulp. It's your turn now! Enjoy.

Yours,

Justin T. O'Conor Sloane

February 2025

PART ONE

THE DOOMED

IN THE END, it was all about the numbers.

The seven worlds were wealthy, there was more than enough for everyone, all twelve billion souls—but the arbitrary logic of electrons wending through labyrinthine circuits decreed otherwise.

The inequities of one set of numbers produced spikes in another set of numbers. In the proudest towers of Earth, thoughtful men and women studied the collisions of the different numbers and worried.

Everywhere the system trembled.

The numbers predicted disaster. If not this calamity, then that catastrophe. Do this and this part collapses. Do that and the other part implodes. Make a choice. Or do nothing at all and hope for the best, that's a choice too, and all the pieces fly apart in ways the numbers can't predict.

Here stood the miraculous city. It rose high above a sunken island, its proud towers sparkling over the restless sea. Within, the managers of the world considered their models and their simulations. They postulated changes and adjustments, then studied the effects that rippled outward, the myriad sufferings that followed, and whether the inevitable could be delayed a little longer.

They were servants of the numbers and they served with guarded loyalty, as well as with envy and resentment. They were not unaware that so much concentrated power had become toxic, its primary product was pain.

If they seemed like gods, it was an illusion. They were merely servants of a higher order. They answered to masters as far removed from them as they were from the lowest laborers in the rice fields.

Above the toils of Terra, in the diamond-speckled darkness, the glitterships sailed, soaring high in the solar winds. Beautiful men and women strolled through cylindrical parks, enjoying the illusion of forests and grasslands—or they floated weightless in opulent salons, savoring the imported tastes of a hundred different traditions, expensive meats and well-aged cheese, exotic fruits and amazing liquors, sweet flavors of all kinds—and not just tobacco and cannabis, but the glorious drugs as well, the fabled hallucinogens and opiates.

They decorated themselves in demonstrations of

wealth. They draped their bodies with confections of luxurious materials, nano-silks and mono-fibers. They adorned their perfect ears and brows, they bejeweled their necks and arms, they splendored themselves with magnificent crowns and pendants—sparkling metalloids, impossible in nature, exquisite jewels that defied the rainbow, all the lavish devices of rarity and wonder. And they reveled in their affluence—they danced and gambled and copulated frantically, obsessively celebrating their elevation. They bound themselves in the twin illusions of success and supremacy, believing that they had achieved not only independence from gravity, but from the worlds that had borne them. "Reality," they laughed, "is what we make it."

Perhaps a few of them knew how fragile their existence had become. There were occasional voices to remind them, voices that were mostly disregarded.

"I'm an old man," said Counselor Jezzro, his eyes twinkling. "I'm well into my sixteenth decade and I have lived twice as long as most people can ever hope to survive. But at a cost. Without an exoskeleton, I can no longer stand in even the slightest gravity. My eyes have been replaced twice and my hearing is almost totally electronic. I am infused with youngblood to keep my heart pumping. But none of this is a victory over entropy as much as it is a delaying action. I doubt I will live long enough to see the next plenary cycle. I've seen too much and too much of what I've seen has given me an intimation of the desperation and despair that the people of Terra are feeling—although I admit I am feeling it from the much more comfortable side."

His listeners were a varied group, drawn from a larger community of ship-borne dilettantes, an heiress or two, a conman, some faded royalty, three billionaires, several political persons in reluctant exile, a drug lord, their respective associates and family members, and a few who were little more than arm-candy. They gave him the respect of listening, but not necessarily agreement.

"I cannot help but notice the contents of your wine glass..." said one of them, a woman of well-constructed elegance. Her name was Sandrossa and she was a princess, an empty title, for neither the monarchy nor the nation which had sanctioned that title existed anymore. Still, she maintained her hereditary claim. "Despite your misgivings, you're drinking the same vintages as those you disparage."

"The wine is here and so am I. I am not an ascetic," Jezzro admitted. "Nevertheless, I fear that the comfortable existence we enjoy is depriving us of the enjoyment of satisfying work. There are days when I miss the warm sunlight on my back. It felt like life. I tended my own garden, you know. As a youngling, I had to learn how to raise my own food. The work was hard, but satisfying—and it was preferable to hunger."

"Work is for workers, any robot can grow a garden," Sandrossa said. "Success is about rising above that, isn't it?"

"Physically, yes, we are above it. Thousands of kilometers above it. But emotionally? Experientially? Wouldn't you agree that our comfortable times here in the glittership have insulated us from the harsher realities of life?"

Sandrossa shrugged. The action would have sent her spinning had she not had one foot anchored in a wall-stirrup. "Well, I for one, am happy to have it be this way. I have no intention of trading places with anyone dirtside."

"Nor would I—unless I could be young again. There are things I miss, particularly the horizontal dance. I am not dark enough to cherish adversity, I merely recognize it as one of the challenges of existence. But I have to wonder about the effects on each of us as individuals as well as a culture—have we become enslaved to our own elevation?"

"Your question makes no sense."

"That's the point, exactly. That there are senses we have willingly abnegated. We took ourselves away from the harshness of planetary life. Have we also walled ourselves away from other aspects? The toils of gravity temper our perceptions. Without them, who are we? Are we gods or monsters?"

At this, Princess Sandrossa laughed aloud. "You must be joking. Monsters don't live like this."

"On that, I fear you may be wrong. You are young,

still only in your seventh decade. You have been well-protected in your wealth, but possibly ill-served. I spend my days doing research, one of the last joys left to me. My body may be failing, but not my mind. And if I am to believe even the smallest part of what is coming from the Seven Worlds, we who live on these beautiful glitterships are not well-perceived. It is a perception rooted in misery. So, yes, I wonder if we have become the unwitting monsters that Terra accuses us of being—that the cost of sustaining our existence up here drains the wealth from below."

"Now you're just being silly, Counselor. Or worse, insane. Their misery is their own doing. I shall hear no more of this subversive prattle." And with that, she deftly unhooked her foot from its stirrup and pushed herself away, aiming with calculated experience for the nearest exit from the salon.

"Now, you've done it," laughed a sleepy-eyed man named Valerian. "You've pissed off the Princess."

"I fear you are correct."

"There will be no end to it, you know. She'll be discussing your implied insult for days to come. Dinners will be insufferable."

Jezzro sighed. "I might have to take meals in my cabin for a week or three—a self-imposed exile from her presence. I don't see a downside. It will give me time to catch up on my reading."

His listeners smiled. They were well-familiar with Princess Sandrossa's pique. Few of them had escaped her occasional fits of wrath. Keeping her lubricated was not an option, she was not a happy drunk.

But even as the Counselor's audience might have sympathized with his appointment to the position of Royal Scapegoat (du jour), they were less inclined to accept the validity of his assertions.

The other listeners included the Lady Daltimore, tall and elegant of visage, the inheritor of a well-tended fortune older than some nations—and her escort, Redmonde, a young man of delicate features. He was exquisitely mannered and as beautiful a boy as one could desire. The Lady had selected him from among several thousand candidates, all of them applicants from the most prestigious universities of five continents. To her, wealth was a divine right.

Beside her, Talent, a dark man with a shining smile, an entrepreneur who had burned through millions to generate billions, his wealth created out of the manipulation of other people's fortunes, with little regard for the consequences to those caught in his wake—and his current trophy, a pale expressionless woman who neither spoke nor smiled. Some speculated that she was merely a simulant, that Talent would not share anything, least of all himself, with any other living soul. Talent had a unique view of affluence—other people's wealth was a resource to be used for his own benefit.

Of them all, perhaps Valerian was the most amenable to uncomfortable ideas. He waved to a passing bot and plucked a drink from its tray. Turning back to Jezzro, he said, "Do you really endorse that agitprop from Terra? Or did you repeat it just to annoy her?"

The Counselor smiled. "A little of each, perhaps. Maybe I am a foolish old man. She isn't the first to accuse me of that. He lifted his hand in a gesture that would have meant peace in an environment of gravity, but only implied a pause in a weightless environment.

"Let me engage in the luxury of pragmatism. We sit at the top of an economic pyramid. We think we are secure, but we depend on the health of the Seven Worlds for our existence. If that pyramid crumbles, we have the farthest to fall. Glittership are crystal goblets, easily shattered. An economic tsunami would turn this flying palace into an airless shell."

Valerian allowed himself a nod of agreement. "And the sun could go nova as well, but I don't see that happening either. You forget, old man, that none of us got here by accident. We are the smart ones. We are the at the top of the economic food chain because we are the fittest." He stopped to correct himself. "We are the most adaptable, the most flexible. I have a contingency plan, I expect that most of the others do too." He looked around the small group. "Am I correct?"

Two or three of the others perched at various points around this corner of the weightless salon murmured their assent, but before Valerian could continue, Jezzro interrupted.

"All very well and good," said the Counselor, "but you might also realize that right here, right now, in this glittership, all of the eggs are in one basket. Not the best plan, you must admit."

Across from Counselor Jezzro, Generalissimo Maximo, a ruler in retirement, no longer waiting for the restoration of his regime, his hasty exile had long since become permanent. Once stocky but now overstuffed, his ruddy flesh glistened in the amber evening. Despite the excellent conditioning of the atmosphere in the salon, he continued to perspire as if he had just finished heaving his bulk up several flights of stairs.

Now, laughing, Generalissimo Maximo put aside the bubble of brandy he had been sucking. "You have survivor's guilt, my friend. Here you are, enjoying the finest of all possible lives, and yet you still cannot allow yourself to be happy."

Jezzro replied slowly. "For myself, yes, I am content. But for our species, no. We have been dancing with disaster for much too long. The misery indices are rising. The tower of inequality is a precarious one, it cannot be built too high without collapsing. The necessary financial instruments will not buttress all the support structures, especially not in a circumstance of increasing uncertainty—"

Maximo laughed louder. "All those numbers,

they are meaningless. If you have enough guns, if you have enough bullets, the numbers don't matter."

"If that were true, you wouldn't be here, would you?" Talent smiled broadly at the Generalissimo.

Maximo frowned, wondering if he had been insulted.

But before he could decide, Talent had already pushed on. "Never underestimate the power of money. Desperate people can be purchased cheap. I think we're safe here. We have well-placed agents throughout the moneysphere—there is no need to speak of guns. It will never come to that."

Counselor Jezzro nodded. "But what happens when there are more desperate men than there is money to buy them off?"

Redmonde, Lady Daltimore's kept-boy, spoke up then. "This is a silly conversation. They cannot reach us here. No one can. That's why we're here." He smiled at the Lady and she patted his hand reassuringly.

Counselor Jezzro offered his own smile as well, an expression tinged with a private amusement. "Perhaps you are right. But if no one can reach you here, then you cannot reach them—this may not be a sanctuary as much as it is a prison."

Redmonde frowned. "All this doom and gloom— you're spoiling the evening. Let's speak of something else."

"You're free to leave, if my conversation disturbs you that much. Princess Sandrossa has already retreated."

Redmonde glanced to the Lady, she gave him no sign of disapproval, so he said, "Your conversation doesn't disturb me. You do. Here you have luxury beyond the wealth of the greatest kings of history and instead of enjoying yourself, you demonstrate that too much knowledge only causes an unpleasant illness of the mind. You exhibit the depressing sadness of the intellectual."

"Ahh, you may be right. Were I as ignorant as you, I could be as blissful as you. But it is late and I am weary—I shall retire now and you may float here in your bubble of luxury, free from the nuisance of thought."

And so it went.

Until the moment it stopped.

When the black destroyers came sleeting out of the shadow cones, it was too late to flee. The glitterships gleamed and sparkled like targets in the darkness. Silent weapons of war flickered across their hulls. Tongues of light blinded the scanners that would have seen and paralyzed the engines that might have fired.

The clank of heavy grapples, the hiss and pop of distant airlocks, then black-armored troops—faceless, dispassionate, methodical, and determined—moved in quickly and secured the central keel. They spread outward, suite by suite, gathering the occupants and herding them rudely into the main salon. Their commands were curt and punctuated with gestures that could only be interpreted as threatening.

Prisoners now, the passengers waited uncomfortably for several hours. They waited without food, without amenities. The golden servants did not come when they were summoned. The liquor-bots remained inactive. The passageways stayed sealed.

The various individuals, still clad in robes and gowns, still not realizing they had been stripped of privilege, still not understanding their situation, shouted at monitors, banged on hatches, demanded to be addressed, puffed themselves up with anger, and promised themselves that this outrage would be sternly dealt with.

When nothing happened, they told each other in reassuring tones that these things take time, so they traded theories—they had been captured by pirates, they were being held for ransom, a pittance really, only a matter of calling their bankers. They called again for the appearance of whatever authority had imprisoned them here. And after a while, it began to sink in. Their captors weren't going to behave like servants.

So they waited.

Lady Daltimore sat silently by herself. She had survived worse, she would survive this. Beside her, lacking that same sense of history and experience, Redmonde sat motionless, seething on her behalf.

Talent found a deck of cards and enrolled Maximo and three others into a game of Martian Poker. Each player received two cards. Two outer cards were dealt face up, Deimos and Phobos. A round of betting, then the three in the well were dealt, to be rolled one at a time. The piece of furniture designed to function as a table was magnetized to hold the cards and the players anchored their feet in convenient stirrups on the bottom so they wouldn't drift away.

"How can you play cards at a time like this?" Redmonde demanded angrily.

"What would you have us do? Worry?" Maximo laughed. "If they shoot us, they shoot us. If they don't, they don't."

"You think they'll shoot us—?"

"Probably not," said Talent. "If they were going to shoot us, they would have done it already. No, they want something. Everybody has a price. We just need to find out what theirs is."

"That's not an answer," Redmonde said.

Talent decided the point wasn't worth pursuing. He turned his attention back to the card game, considered a moment, then pushed his cards in. His rule was simple. Hesitation is a reason to fold.

Maximo dealt the next hand and they played in silence, speaking only to call or raise.

Frustrated at being ignored, impatient for something to happen, Redmonde swept the salon, as if looking for an answer, or escape. "Hey!" he cried, abruptly. "Where's the old man?"

Maximo and Talent both glanced up from their game. Others looked around as well.

"You mean the Counselor?" said Talent.

"Yeah. Him. Where is he?"

"You just now noticed that he's missing? I noticed it an hour ago."

"Why didn't you say anything?" demanded Redmonde.

"What was the percentage? We already had enough to worry about."

"Perhaps our hosts invited him to do the vacuum dance." Maximo chuckled. "Perhaps they didn't like what he had to say any more than our young friend."

Talent shook his head. He glanced at his cards and folded. "There's no percentage in that either."

"Eh?"

"If I was a betting man—and I am—I'd bet that he's been having a nice little chat with them."

"You think so?"

"He's that kind of man. He likes to be the wisdom in the room. He's probably talking their ears off right now."

"You have no proof of that—"

Talent began ticking points off on his fingers. "It only takes ten minutes, fifteen at most, to secure a ship—" Before Maximo could interrupt, he explained, "Simulations. If you want to capture a ship, you have to threaten to destroy it. You can't dock with a ship that dances around, so you have to be willing to carry out your threat if they refuse to be boarded. The Captain of the target ship knows this. So he has a choice, death or surrender. Surrender is the better option. You can be ransomed. Nobody ransoms the dead. So—once the ships are docked, it only takes ten minutes, fifteen at most, for the boarding party to assume control. After that, it's a matter of sweeping for prisoners."

He went to the next finger. "It takes maybe another twenty or thirty minutes to herd all the passengers to the salon. Notice the crew aren't here. They're being held somewhere else, probably the galley, or else they're secured in their quarters. So the crew aren't the targets, we are. Still following?"

Talent touched the tip of his third finger. "If they were planning to execute any of us, they would have started immediately. That they have not killed any of us means they have some other plan. So, do the math. They've seized the ship, they've moved passengers and crew to holding spaces. Maybe add some time for them to report to whoever they have to report to. They needed less than an hour to do all that. The vessel is secured. Now what? We've been here in this salon, waiting, for nearly three. So—"

The fourth finger. "—Whatever their plan, their actions are contingent on the circumstances. And that means that someone and someone, probably several someones, are having a discussion. And because Jezzro isn't in this chamber, that means he's most likely in that other place, probably the Captain's cabin or whatever passes for a briefing room, where all those someones are having their discussion."

"You think he's collaborating—?" Redmonde said.

"Of course not. That's not his style. I think he's negotiating."

"Only cowards negotiate," said Redmonde.

Maximo chuckled, but Talent laughed out loud.

"You mock me, sir?"

"Of course, not. I mock your ignorance."

Redmonde scowled, but Lady Daltimore placed a hand on his forearm and whatever reply he might have been composing, his words remained unspoken.

Maximo turned to Talent, their card game forgotten for the moment. "Allow me?"

"Of course." Talent nodded.

In an environment of gravity, Talent would have leaned back in his chair. Here, he simply shifted his posture, turning to give himself a wider field of vision.

Maximo focused on Redmonde. "You negotiate when you have something the other party desires enough to negotiate for—because negotiation is easier than force. I speak from ugly experience. Violence is expensive. You draw your weapon only when you have no other options. So if Counselor Jezzro is negotiating, then there is something our captors want from us that they cannot achieve any other way—and certainly not by killing us."

Redmonde glanced to his patron, she gave him no sign of disapproval, so he said, "But the Counselor has no right to negotiate on our behalf. No one here has authorized him to do so."

Talent smiled. "If our captors have authorized him, your objection is irrelevant."

"Well, whatever they decide, it's invalid. We haven't agreed to it. He has no right to give up anything that doesn't belong to him. If he wants to give away his own property—"

"He has no property—"

"Then how did he get here—?"

"He is here for his health, not his wealth," said Talent. "You haven't done your research. It's a reward for service and an investment in his continuing value. His patrons want the benefits of his wisdom for as long as his body can survive."

"He could have had augments—"

"He's outlived his augments. You can only do so much with bionics. The point is that somebody felt it a worthwhile expense to have him here. The Counselor has always had a reputation for insight and analysis. His participation in our conversations has not been solely for our benefit, but for his patrons' as well. I am convinced that when he retires to his cabin, pleading exhaustion, he takes time to note his observations. Certainly, he does not do that for his own benefit alone."

"So he's been spying on us all along?" Redmonde said, angrily.

"Are you that naïve?" asked Talent. "Did you really think we were exempt out here? He came right out and said it, more than once, that we are not immune to the circumstances of the Seven Worlds.

Of course, they're watching us. If not the Counselor, then certainly the crew of this glittership. Probably all of them. I doubt you can fart without a dozen intelligence agencies annotating their files on what you had for lunch."

"Let them listen all they want. I've done nothing wrong," said Redmonde. "I've earned my place."

"Of course, you have," said Maximo with a patronizing air. "And a very lovely place it is. I can only compliment the Lady on her exquisite taste in companions. You must have some particular talent far beyond your conversational skills. I know that I and my friends here have found many of your comments delightfully amusing."

Mollified by Maximo's apparent validation of his abilities, Redmonde fell silent—then he frowned as the suspicion crept up on him that he'd just been eloquently insulted, but by the time he was certain it was too late to respond. Maximo and Talent had returned their attentions to their card game with the other passengers.

In a quieter tone, Maximo asked Talent, "What do you think he is negotiating?"

"Not our lives, that's for certain."

"Our fortunes?"

"Our futures, I expect." Talent hesitated, considering his next words. "Several hours ago, the economic congress agreed to hold hearings on financial restructure."

"It will never pass—" snorted Maximo. "We own the votes to keep anything we want locked up in committee."

"Perhaps. Perhaps not. But the congress had to show they were doing something, so they authorized a freeze—to keep people like ourselves from moving our accounts to safer havens while they debate what to do with our money. Even if the restructure goes nowhere, they have still demonstrated their ability to take our fortunes."

"You think too much," said Maximo. He meant it as a joke, but it was an uncomfortable one. "How long will the freeze last?"

Talent shrugged. "Hard to say. A week? A year? Until the riots start? I hope you were wise enough to spread your fortune into many separate places."

Maximo didn't answer. His expression went sour.

Lady Daltimore had been listening quietly to the entire exchange. Now, she straightened and drifted deliberately closer. Even in micro-gravity, the lady managed an elegant bearing. "Monsieur Talent, you seem to have more experience with this kind of affair than you have previously admitted. So tell us, if these pirates do not need us for ransom, then what do they want us for?"

"Symbols, dear lady. Symbols. I believe they wish to parade us through the streets of Paris in tumbrels."

Lady Daltimore frowned. "And what would that accomplish?"

Talent smiled. "It's the third act. The death of Lear. It's about seeing the king stripped of power, humbled and reduced to a miserable state, a final soliloquy of pain and remorse."

"It won't work," said Maximo, folding his arms in a gesture of defiance.

"Oh, it'll work, all right," said Talent. "The howling mob will be satisfied—it's part of the process."

Lady Daltimore remained unimpressed. "Nonsense. It will never happen."

"I doubt we'll have a choice."

"We are not the kind of people who give in to mobs."

"You think we are not?" Talent shook his head. "We are no different, no different at all. We are all of us the same, we are walking bags of water—eating, shitting, and fucking our lives away for as long as we can—until finally, one day we give up our water. We all die. Some of us die afraid. Some of us die exhausted. But all of us die."

"Perhaps you do not understand who I am—my family, my position. They won't dare touch me. You, perhaps. But I am above that. My name means dignity. I will never surrender that."

"Nor should you," replied Talent. "Many of those who rode in tumbrils held their dignity to the end, they didn't know how to behave otherwise. Others were simply puzzled, wondering what they had done to deserve such a fate, so they bent into the guillotine more confused than afraid, expecting at any moment to discover this was all some kind of a grand charade. But yes, most of the condemned were resigned to their end. Some sagged in despair, others shrieked in terror and begged for mercy—but by the time the tumbrils rolled, they all knew what lay at the end of that too-short journey. But it wasn't for them—it was for the mob. It was their humbling that the mob sought. It was their terror that the mob enjoyed. The terror—remember that. The more the better. The mob fed on it. Every one of them, trapped in a dead-end existence, this was their only taste of power—the power to hurt back."

"You sound like you agree with the mob," said Maximo.

Talent laughed. "On the contrary. I am here in the sky—not down there in the dirt. That should tell you where my priorities are. That I can speak so candidly demonstrates only that I understand how the system works—not to be a victim of it, but a master."

"And if it happens that you have been correct in your analysis, then what outcome may we expect here—?"

"That, my friend, depends on how persuasive a negotiator our good Counselor may be."

Talent's speculations were not far from wrong. Nor did he and his fellow passengers have much longer to wait.

The hatch to the salon popped open and three black-armored troops entered, followed by a woman in a black jumpsuit, Counselor Jezzro, and two more troops. The woman was dark-skinned, possibly a mix of African and Arab, but she had Chinese in her ancestry as well. Her shining black hair was cropped short.

Immediately, various individuals about the cabin began demanding answers from her. "Who are you people?" "What do you want from us?" "What's going on here?" "When will you free us?" "I demand a lawyer." "I need access to my office." And "You'll never get away with this."

Ignoring all these remarks, the woman gestured to her second-in-command. He and the other troops began herding everyone to the far end of the salon while she and the Counselor settled themselves near the primary passageway. She secured a tablet to another free-fall table, arranging it so she was the only person who could see its screen.

When all was settled, she raised a hand for silence—and waited.

Most of the prisoners were more accustomed to giving orders than receiving them, they did not recognize any authority but their own, so it took a while for them to realize that they were in an unfamiliar situation.

Finally, satisfied that her authority had been acknowledged, the woman spoke. "I am Captain Mondrait of the Unified Command Authority—"

"Never heard of it," snorted a fat man. "We don't recognize you or your—"

He didn't get to finish. The tranquilizer dart hit the side his neck and his sentence ended with a gurgle. One of the troops pushed himself across the room to float the immobilized man out a rear passage.

"If there are no further interruptions," Captain Mondrait said, "I will continue. I am Captain Mondrait of the Unified Command Authority. As of thirteen hundred hours, Greenwich Mean Time, the Unified Command Authority has been empowered to act as the enforcement arm of the Economic Restructuring Act—"

She held up her hand again to forestall any objections. "The act was passed in secret session, twenty-one days ago. Enforcement agencies have been moving into place ever since. This ship and all her passengers are now under the judicial authority granted to me by the Unified Command. Let me clarify that for all of you. It is not just your assets that have been impounded.

"All of you, individuals as well as corporate entities, are now being held under the authority of this act and the disposition of your properties as well as your individual fates will be determined by the proceedings of this judicial body, of which I am the presiding member. There will be no appeals allowed beyond this chamber.

"Charges have been filed against the Captain of this vessel, every member of the crew, and every passenger, regardless of circumstance. All of you are under indictment for the criminal appropriation of wealth."

She waited until the uproar faded again to silence, and after the tranquilized bodies of two more passengers had been removed.

"I do not care one way or the other," Captain Mondrait said. "Whether or not you recognize the authority of this court, this court still has the authority.

"You will each be given a choice. You can demand a leniency hearing aboard this ship—or you can accept the sentence already pronounced. Yes, you heard correctly. You have all been tried in absentia and found guilty by the judicial agencies of the United Command Authority. The evidence was compelling beyond a reasonable doubt.

"Each and every one of you has been convicted. Your presence aboard this ship would have been evidence enough of guilt—the use of extreme wealth for personal aggrandizement, but the court examined all of your actions, all of your holdings, before pronouncing sentence. If you choose to return to Earth, there will be no possibility of leniency. Those sentences have been reviewed and appeal has been denied. The mood on Earth is not very forgiving right now.

"Or…you can accept the authority of this body and accept a penalty somewhat less severe. For most of you, that would be permanent exile on any of the seven worlds, except Earth. You will not have the lives you are accustomed to. You will not have access to your illicit wealth. You will have to work for your survival, but you will survive."

Talent and Maximo exchanged glances. "It could be worse," said Talent.

Maximo agreed, "Survival is always an opportunity."

"Better than the alternative."

As if she could hear them, Captain Mondrait spoke up. "You will have to demonstrate some skills that are marketable. Otherwise, you will be assigned unskilled labor. So you might want to check your educational and experiential resumes."

Now, she nodded toward Counselor Jezzro who had floated silently and grimly beside her this whole time. "In your favor, you are fortunate to have had Counselor Jezzro aboard. Although he is also under indictment, he has already demonstrated his value as a consultant to this court. All of you should be grateful that he has offered persuasive arguments for leniency. Counselor?"

Jezzro spoke softly, but his voice was amplified so that everyone could hear it clearly. "I did not ask to be a party to these proceedings. I am a reluctant participant."

He paused to clear his throat, his voice was uneven. "Captain Mondrait showed me the transcripts of the court hearings on Earth. According to the simulations and models, the United Command Authority had no choice but to authorize a surgical response against the criminal appropriation of wealth. It is their position that the economic body of the Earth and her dependent worlds has been paralyzed by crippling instability caused by severe economic inequality—too much wealth has been concentrated in too few hands.

"The immediate solution is to remove those individuals and institutions that have been functioning as parasites on the economic body as quickly as possible and to put the impounded wealth back into circulation at the lowest possible levels where the resultant liquidity will create a term of recovery, thus providing a window of opportunity to allow for a longer-term restructuring of the economic system that created the circumstances of parasitism in the first place.

"Yes, I know some of you will find that offensive, but that is the terminology of the court that has pronounced sentence on all of us and we need to be aware that is how we are perceived by a majority of the twelve billion members of our species. Whether you believe that is an accurate characterization or not—it is irrelevant. We are long past that argument.

"Captain Mondrait has the authorization to carry out the sentences that were issued by the United Command Authority on Earth. Those were death sentences. She could have destroyed this vessel with a single missile. She chose not to.

"Were she a less compassionate individual, had

she chosen to act injudiciously, all of us would have been sent out the nearest airlock within moments of her seizure of this vessel. That did not happen—partly because Captain Hallman demanded that guarantee before allowing her ship to dock, but mostly because Captain Mondrait does not believe in wasting either property or lives. I believe we can be grateful for that much."

Jezzro paused then to catch his breath. The long unpleasant speech had taken its toll. After a moment, he resumed. "I did not choose to be a voice in this situation. My participation is reluctant. But I have argued as persuasively as I can that there is much value aboard this vessel, and that each and every one of us can still demonstrate an ability to contribute to the well-being of the seven worlds. Because we have several days before this ship can be brought back to low-Earth orbit, Captain Mondrait has agreed to use some of that time to review individual cases. I have agreed to act as a consultant, a liaison—an advocate."

Captain Mondrait spoke then. "Thank you, Counselor. I hope that you are correct that your fellow passengers here will accept these circumstances much more readily hearing it from you than from me."

She shifted her position to face the rest of the group. "Let me be clear. I will offer leniency only when and where it has been justified as an appropriate mitigation. I will not be bullied. I will not listen to demands. I will listen only to opportunities for reparation. That will be all for now. A schedule of hearings will be posted shortly. You may return to your cabins, but do not call for service. The crew has been sequestered. If you wish to eat, you will serve yourselves in the galley. All other services are suspended. Thank you for making this far less unpleasant than I expected it to be."

And with that, she left. Her troops pushed themselves through the hatch after her and the passengers were alone again.

The uproar began immediately. Some wept, some raged, some sat stunned, unable to speak. One or two screamed incoherently, their tumbled emotions paralyzing all thought. Several began arguing with anyone who wouldn't push themselves away. One or two began calculating. A few fled to their cabins, where they discovered that most of their personal belongings had already been removed.

Although Captain Mondrait's orders were to strip the glittership of its opulent furnishings, all the way down to its bare bulkheads, she chose to delay the implementation of that action until she could take a proper inventory. As she inspected the vessel, she became increasingly appalled at the waste of wealth, the squandering of power, the appropriation of resources. What she was seeing was far beyond what she had expected. This was beyond criminal. There were no words for this monstrous luxury.

She began to regret listening to Counselor Jezzro, allowing herself to be persuaded by his arguments for leniency. "Most of these people don't know any better," he had said. "They've lived inside a bubble of privilege for so long they are completely disassociated from the harsher realities of life. Perhaps a greater punishment than death would be to confront them with what they have denied for so long. Give them the lives they've earned, not the lives they've purchased."

It had seemed a worthy approach—but now, as she surveyed the passages, her heart hardened. These panels along this passage—these rare woods had been stripped from the last surviving rain forests. The golden fittings—the ore had been dug out of the earth by men and women scrabbling to earn enough to buy a bowl of rice. The drugs in the cabinets—the lives of a thousand children could have been saved with these unused medicines. And the air—it was perfumed with the rarest and most elusive of scents, Captain Mondrait didn't recognize the flavors but the readout on her tablet identified every item with annoying accuracy and reported the true costs of what she was seeing.

The numbers terrified her. She could have fed a nation with the wealth concentrated here. She was almost afraid to survey the contents of the galley. The gluttony of these people was astonishing. What horrors would she find in the kitchens? Whole ecosystems had gone extinct for the encapsulated greed of this ship.

And this was not the only vessel. Elsewhere,

other crews were boarding other glitterships and other Captains were facing the same discoveries and dilemmas. She almost envied those who were simply following orders. Compassion had become an unbearable burden.

She decided to start with the easiest. It violated her own rule—eat the frog first, get it over with and move on—but she needed time to understand. Somewhere, deep inside herself, she still believed in justice as the most human of all endeavors. This mission, however, was sorely testing that belief.

What justice was possible for those who were responsible for the rape of the planet? What justice is there for the millions suffering disease, poverty, and hunger? What justice is there for the children denied the opportunities that come with healthy parents, education, and a chance to reach adulthood? Suddenly, all the diatribes and screeds that Captain Mondrait had only half-listened to—abruptly, all those words had real meaning to her. She wavered between being dispirited and resolved.

No matter what she decided here, it would not make enough of a difference. It would not mend the past. It would not save the future. If anything at all, it would be a momentary salve for the spirits of those who had been most severely wounded.

The Captain had been warned of what she would discover, but even with all the briefings, she was still unprepared for the emotional impact. She felt herself becoming angry—radicalized by her passion.

Yes, these were human beings here—Counselor Jezzro had been right about that. But they were failures at being human. They were the beneficiaries of greed, of hedonism, of gluttony and selfishness. They were the ultimate spoiled children of their generation.

And those who served them—the captain and crew of this glittership—they could not be excused as mere enablers. They were co-conspirators. They had applied their skills to the maintenance of this flying palace and they benefited in turn from the wealth they attended. What would be a fitting punishment for them?

Perhaps the singular order from her superiors would be the best. Execute them all and be done with it. Elsewhere, aboard other ships, other Captains were sentencing their captives to the airlock dance—and probably without much introspection. Perhaps they were able to disassociate duty from thought.

But Captain Mondrait suffered from the dual conditions of empathy and wisdom. She was painfully aware of the peculiar irony of this situation. Her ship and her crew were as far removed from the circumstances of poverty as the people they were arresting. The cost of an attack vessel was even more than the cost of a glittership and the burden of its construction was borne not by the wealthy who had created a myriad of ways to recuse themselves from taxes, but by those who had not the resources to evade. She was a creature of privilege herself, albeit of a more severe design.

Such is the paradox of any revolution. While any revolution is authorized by an angry mob, the leaders of the movement are almost always refugees from the same privilege, paradoxically educated and disaffected, and ultimately closer in spirit to those they rebel against than those they set out to lead.

It was the gap between ideology and practice that troubled Captain Mondrait—but at the same time, she also understood that a failure on her part to be as severe as circumstances demanded would be interpreted by her superiors as complicity, or worse—sympathy. Despite the persuasiveness of Counselor Jezzro's pleas, she realized she had far less choice in the outcome than she might have wished.

In the end, it came down to allocation of resources—the coldest equation of all. What contribution could any of these individuals create for the greater good that would justify any further investment of resources? She would need to be convinced.

The hearings did not go quickly. There was a lot of posturing, a lot of self-righteousness, a lot of explanation, a lot of justification, a lot of useless conversation—and way too much ignorance.

When Lady Daltimore patiently, as if talking to a child, explained at length the contributions of her family, all of the various industries they had funded and how they had improved the quality of life for everyone on the planet—and that they had amassed great fortunes in the process—well, that wealth was simply the justly earned rewards for their efforts, a tool to create more industry and more wealth, and really nothing more than a pittance compared to all of the wealth they had created for so many others, including the technological progress that had raised the standard of life for so many—well, therefore the perpetrators of this illegal and ultimately ill-fated attempt to create a collectivist tyranny should be grateful to her family and to all of the other families that had made all of this glory possible—and in addition, she personally felt insulted that anyone representing this criminal gang of political illiterates should dare to sit in judgment of her—it was at that moment that Captain Mondrait finally lost the last of her patience.

But she didn't let it show.

"Are you quite finished," she asked.

Lady Daltimore said, "I have a great deal more to say. But if you are not going to listen, I am not obligated to educate you."

"Ah, yes. You're finished. I have one question for you."

The Lady waited.

"Is there anything you can contribute to the society that supports you that justifies any further expenditures in maintaining your existence?"

"The question is irrelevant. I have already earned my privilege."

"Your privilege is a thing of the past. That past has expired and your privilege with it. We are now talking about your future. Is there anything you can contribute that justifies keeping you alive?"

"I do not recognize your authority to sit in judgment of my value."

"I'll take that as a no."

"As well you should."

"So be it." Captain Mondrait looked to Counselor Jezzro. "Counselor?"

Had there been gravity in the salon, he would have sagged. Instead he shook his head. "I have nothing to offer here."

Captain Mondrait turned back to Lady Daltimore. "You have been charged with the criminal appropriation of wealth to the detriment of society. The tragedy here is that you are apparently incapable of recognizing anything outside of your own selfish bubble of privilege. You remain stubbornly unaware that you are existing as a parasite. You are ignorant of the damage that you have caused to the health of the multi-global economy. In addition, you have failed to demonstrate any mitigating value for your continued existence. Therefore, I have no choice but to order that the sentence of the United Command Authority be carried out with expedience. There is no avenue of appeal. As a condition of mercy, this court will give you six hours to compose any final messages to be forwarded to loved ones, if any."

Captain Mondrait banged her gavel, an action that would have sent her shooting away from the table she was using as a desk, had she not firmly anchored her feet in its stirrups. "Next case," she said.

Lady Daltimore stiffened. "You have no right—"

Ordinarily, Captain Mondrait would not have replied. But this time, she gave herself permission. If she could have stood up in weightlessness, she would have. Instead, she straightened enough to rise above the table. "I wish it were so, Lady Daltimore, that I had not been given this authority—but I have been. I have taken an oath that I would carry out my duties as an officer of the United Command Authority, and while integrity may be an unfamiliar experience for you, it is not such a casual relationship for me. I intend to keep my oath and carry out my orders, no matter how unpleasant that task may be. And as unpleasant as this will be for you, I assure you the consequences will be far more unpleasant for me. Because I will have to live with my decision, you will not." To her second, she said, "Take her away."

As the Lady's protests faded down the passage, Captain Mondrait turned to Counselor Jezzro. "Do not look at me that way. Yes, I will admit I enjoyed telling her off—and I hate myself for enjoying it. Maybe it's not her fault that she's an ignorant, spoiled brat in a grownup body—maybe the blame should fall on those who raised her to be that. But they're not here and she is—and even as I hate her, I regret hating her for making me hate her. Does that make sense?"

"Perfectly."

"You have not made my job easier, you know."

"You asked for wisdom, not comfort."

"Next time, I'll know better. How are you holding up, sir? Do you need a break?"

Counselor Jezzro lowered his voice and leaned in. "I am far less fragile than I pretend to be. But you already know that."

"If you are trying to make a case for your own survival..."

"Of course, I am. Everything a human being does is self-serving. Altruism is an illusion."

"You think so?"

"Do you think your task here is anything else?"

"I'll have to defer that discussion for another time." She nodded toward a sudden noise emanating from the passageway. Two troops pushed a very angry and somewhat disheveled young man into the salon—Lady Daltimore's erstwhile aide and companion, Redmonde.

He came in shouting, twisting in the air, bouncing off a wall, flailing and grabbing, trying to orient himself and failing badly. "You vile bitch!" he shouted. "You have no right to kill her! She's done nothing wrong! She's a good person! She—she—" His voice cracked into a sob. "Please don't do it, please! I'm begging you. She's all I have. She hasn't done anything wrong. I should know. She just minds her own business, mostly. We only came here for a little while, a vacation, a getaway from all the troubles below—we didn't know, how could we, but please—"

Captain Mondrait waited patiently until exhausted, Redmonde finally fell silent.

"Are you quite finished?" she asked.

He shook his head, thought better, then nodded. "I ask for mercy. Not for me, but for Lady Daltimore."

"Hmm," said Captain Mondrait. She looked to Jezzro.

"An unselfish act," the Counselor noted. "I have to admit it is unexpected."

"She's his patron. Without her, he's poor again. What was that you were saying about altruism? What was the word you used? An illusion?"

"You have me there," Jezzro admitted.

Mondrait turned back to Redmonde. "It's a question of contribution. What value can you bring to the world? The world nurtured you, educated you, even gave you opportunities—"

"Lady Daltimore gave me the opportunities. Not you, not the world."

"Ahh, there's where you are mistaken. You were raised in privilege, you were educated in privilege. Without that privilege, you would have been nothing and the Lady would never have noticed you. But never mind, that's irrelevant. The question before us is not the past, but the future. What value can you provide to the world, what contribution can you make? If it is sufficiently valuable, I will include the Lady in your pardon—but it had better be remarkable. What will you contribute that justifies you having a future?"

Redmonde didn't answer. After a bit, he said, "I don't understand the question."

Mondrait nodded. "I'm not surprised. Contribution to others is an alien concept to you, isn't it."

"I know what contribution is."

"Ahh, then we're making progress. What kind of contribution can you make? What skills have you developed? What can you give back to Terra?"

"Why should I give anything at all? What has Terra ever done for me?"

Mondrait raised an eyebrow. She looked to Jezzro. "Do you want to answer that?"

Jezzro shook his head. "I've already had this conversation. Several times. It goes nowhere."

Mondrait turned back to Redmonde. "What has Terra ever done for you? Here you are, healthy, well-fed, well-educated, living a life far beyond the means of almost every other living human being—and you have to ask what Terra has ever done for you?"

"I did it myself. No one did it for me. I earned my place here by my own effort. I serve the Lady Daltimore. That's my contribution."

"That relationship is over. Very soon, the Lady Daltimore will have no further need of your services. So, in the absence of her patronage, who or what will you serve?"

"No one. I've served enough. It is my turn to be served."

"Wrong answer, Redmonde. You still fail to understand. You say you did it all yourself? Did you build the university you attended? Did you train the instructors who taught you? Or shall I make it even simpler for you? Did you build the house you lived in? Did you build the vehicles that carried you? Did you grow the crops that fed you? Did you sew your own clothes? Cut your own hair? Did you do your own laundry? Even make your own meals? No, none of that. You have been served all your life. Now it is your turn to serve. What will you contribute to others?"

"Nothing. Nothing at all. Let them make their own way as I've made mine."

"Your way? You've been a mite living on a parasite. I'm giving you the opportunity to become a working human being. Are you smart enough to take it?"

"I'm smart enough to know that you are a petty bureaucrat, carrying out the orders of a greater tyranny. I won't cooperate."

"Ahh, I see—but you're not smart enough to convince this court that your life is worth something."

Mondrait reached for her gavel, but before she could pronounce sentence, Jezzro whispered to her. "Yes, he's an ass. But—"

"But what?"

"He's young. He's stupid. He never had a chance to learn better."

"You think he's worth saving?"

"We were all young and stupid once. Most of us outgrew it."

Mondrait sighed. She turned back to Redmonde. "I could send you back to Terra. Perhaps they can find something useful for you to do."

Redmonde shrugged. "Terra had no use for me. I have no use for Terra."

"So you say, but you seem to forget that you are a child of Terra."

"I've heard the speech. Child of Terra? I don't believe it. That's what slaves tell each other. We're all in this together. We have to work together. We have to share. We have to be one big crappy family. Well, the only thing conversation ever accomplished was to keep people comfortable in their poverty. You want more? Try this one. The smart people work their way up. If they want to stop being poor, they should work harder."

Mondrait and Jezzro exchanged a look. Mondrait bent her head and whispered, "I think in this case, young and stupid may be a terminal condition."

"I fear you're right," Jezzro whispered back. "Nevertheless…"

"Yes. Nevertheless." She returned her attention to Redmonde. "I have to make a choice here. The easy choice would be to let you accompany the Lady. I could do that with a clear conscience. But I wonder if there might be a better path. You owe a debt to Terra—"

"Like hell I do. Terra be damned. All I ever wanted was to get away from Terra. If I never hear that name again, it will still be too soon."

Mondrait's expression hardened. Her eyes narrowed, her lips tightened. She took a deep breath and reached again for the gavel—

"Grant his wish," said Jezzro.

She stopped. She looked at the Counselor.

"Let that be his contribution—"

"I don't—" And then she did. "Oh. I see."

To Redmonde, she said. "Are you certain of that?"

"Certain of what?"

"That you never want to hear the name of Terra again."

"Oh hell, yes. Goddamn Terra. Goddamn that whole rotten world!" Redmonde cried, "Goddamn every speck of her earth and air. Goddamn her continents and her oceans. Goddamn her people and her cities and her wars. Goddamn everything about her. I never want to hear the name of Terra again. And that goes for all the Seven Worlds. Damn them all to hell. They've done nothing for me, I want nothing from them. Is that clear enough?"

"Yes, it is. It certainly is." Mondrait held her gavel ready. "Do you have anything else to say before I pronounce sentence?"

"Screw Terra."

"Is that it?"

"Yes. No. Screw Terra twice."

Mondrait nodded. "Thank you. You make my job easier. Redmonde, you have been a part of the cancer that has fed on the wealth of the Seven Worlds. You have shared its gluttony. Because you cooperated with that greed, you are guilty of its perseverance. You have been given ample opportunity to repent. You have not.

"Therefore, it is the judgment of this court that you shall be excised from the society of free men and women. You shall be exiled from all of the worlds of the human community. You shall never again set foot on any of the Seven Worlds, neither shall you ever hear the names of any of the Seven Worlds, nor shall you hear any news of any of the Seven Worlds—and in particular you shall never hear the name of Terra again, nor shall you hear any news of Terra. You shall be stripped of your name and your history. From this moment on, you will have no human identity. You will have no human connections. You will be known solely as the man without a planet."

"Ha!" Redmonde laughed. "You think that's a punishment—?"

"What I think is irrelevant. You, however, will have a lifetime to consider it." She motioned to her aides. "Take him away. We're adjourned." She banged the gavel—hard.

PART TWO

THE DAMNED

THE GLITTERSHIPS STILL sailed among the seven worlds. There were goods to be manufactured and shipped. There was commerce to be done. There were economies to be maintained.

And if one were cynical enough, one could argue that nothing had changed except the justifications and the people making them.

But, this time around, enough of the wealth and enough of the privilege was available to enough of the people that revolution receded to resentment. Resentment was inevitable, human beings are hardwired that way.

As for Redmonde, he was made comfortable. He had a cabin on the clockwise rotating wheel. He had a semblance of gravity. It was only a small cabin at the far end of the crew quarters, it had no windows, only a wall screen, but it wasn't a prison cell. He was provided for.

He was given simple meals, healthy enough, and he could use the gymnasium when it was closed to others. His screen had only a limited access. He could not access any news or popular entertainments, nothing that referred to any of the Seven Worlds. He could listen to instrumental music, but even that was limited. He could read or view only the most disassociated adventures. He had everything necessary to for a comfortable physical survival, but he was denied all knowledge of life beyond.

And if that could be all he wanted, then he wanted for nothing.

But what he didn't have was human contact, not even the simplest adventures of connection.

It should have been a life without stress—without the eternal jockeying for status that had amused Lady Daltimore. Her fascination with the chessboard of human relationships, the manipulations of position and power gave her a savage purpose.

His assistance had been valuable to her. He had shared gossip with the other attendants, and occasional sexual dalliances to gain even more intimate gossip. Lady Daltimore gave him bits and pieces to share with his bedmates, and in return, they shared more candidly than they should have, information that he always brought back to his patron.

Redmonde served as her eyes and ears to the

underside of the glittership. He assumed that the other attendants did the same and so in his own way, he knew he had his own place on the chessboard.

But now, removed from that society, he floated in a vacuum.

At first he found it relaxing, almost peaceful.

Then dull.

Then frustrating.

He missed the game, the challenge, the momentary importance.

From time to time, the glittership would orbit one of the worlds. He had no portholes, his screens would not give him any information at all, and he had no skill in determining his whereabouts based on travel times across the system.

Those were the times when he was transferred from one ship to the next. Whatever the reasons for the transfers, no one ever said. He was moved politely, dispassionately, without comment. The few times he tried to ask for news of any kind, the answer was always the same, silence.

The accommodations were equivalent. A small space, no better than anything reserved for the lowest crew. Never better, but never worse. A cabin. Access to exercise and meals and occasionally a walk around the common decks.

But never any contact with anyone who might speak of the Seven Worlds.

Never.

His mind, always active, explored the possibilities of escape.

There were none.

Failing that, he wondered if he could bargain some advantage, but he had nothing to bargain with. No information, no position, no advantage at all. And there was nothing to bargain for. There was nothing that he wanted—nothing possible. The old ways were gone.

Perhaps he might plead his case to someone, perhaps he might achieve some exile less…less boring. But there was no one to whom he could plead. There was no one who had the authority even to listen.

He lost track of time. He was forbidden even a calendar. And from one glittership to the other, the concepts of day and night evaporated.

He could have complained about the food. None of it aspired to the elegance he had grown used to, but there was no one to complain to. They met his assertions with silence and blank expressions.

He could have complained about his cabin, the texture of his sheets, the commonness of his clothes, the rudeness of his surroundings. But again, there was no one who would listen.

He existed. He endured.

And once he even came close to weeping. But he would not give *them* even that much satisfaction. He knew they were watching. He knew they were laughing. He knew they were taking pleasure in his solitary existence.

He had to believe that.

Because if the reverse were true, if they had forgotten him, if they were ignoring him, then the circumstances of his exile were even more terrible.

Finally, he asked for a keyboard. He began to write. He knew they had to be reading his words, he didn't care. He wrote about the luxuries he missed. He wrote about the lavish meals. He wrote about the black silk pantaloons he wore, the scarlet tunic with the Daltimore crest, the embroidered robes he wore in attendance at the holiest rituals.

He wrote about Lady Daltimore and her skillful maneuvers through the world of elegance. He wrote about her dalliances, both political and sexual. He wrote about his own services as well, and her extraordinary adventures both in bed and out. He went on at some length about the various low-grav adventures that she enjoyed—and how he and others often performed for her amusement.

He wrote about his own sexual adventures with the attendants of the other elites. He wrote about the gossip they shared—the gossip they were supposed to share and the gossip they were forbidden to acknowledge.

He didn't care who read it or what they might think. He wrote because he had nothing else to do. Just recording it gave him satisfaction.

Occasionally, he wrote of his frustrations, of the injustices he was forced to endure. He wrote about what he missed, the delicacies he would like to enjoy again. But even in the writing, he could savor them in memory, so he wrote about them at length. And sometimes, he wrote what fates he imagined for others, what destinies he wanted to condemn them to. He wrote about the things that still festered in his soul, especially those people who had inflicted pain on him, whether unwittingly or deliberate. He wrote about those who had attempted to betray him, and those who might have succeeded. He wrote about those who had ignored him and neglected him. He wrote about those who had never acknowledged his many ways of demonstrating excellence. He wrote about his position, his importance, his value, all the skills he brought to the elites that were now being wasted in this silly stupid permanent exile that must be costing millions and ultimately served no purpose at all.

He believed—he had to believe—that his words were being read, being considered, being understood, that perhaps he had a following on the Seven Worlds, people who identified with him, felt for him, might someday rescue him, or even simply petition for his parole, anything.

The one thing he didn't write, he couldn't write, he wouldn't give them that satisfaction, was his...he didn't have a word for it...something he felt, something that gnawed at him. Remorse? No, that couldn't be it. Regret. Well, maybe. No, not regret. It wasn't his fault that the elites had been so blind they'd allowed a revolution. He'd served them well. He'd believed in them. They understood…something. Some people were meant to lead. And leaders deserved to live well. They took on the responsibilities of leadership. And those who served them, who made it all possible, they deserved their perquisites as well. No, he had nothing to regret. He had served well.

The revolutionaries—they were the evil ones. They had been arbiters of judgment and death. They had created misery. They had ended the magnificence of elegance, the celebration of excellence, and replaced it with a common ugliness, the crudeness of mere existence. What shallow people they were.

He wrote that as well.

He came to his own understanding.

It didn't matter.

Nothing mattered.

He wasn't going to be paroled. He wasn't ever going to escape this existence. So he might as well write what he saw, what he felt, what he believed, what he knew, what was so—and what was so in his existence was the enormous indignity, the deliberate persecution, the need of the new regime to have people to punish. He was merely another of their unfortunate victims.

At least, however, they had spared him his life, and he would write this, his courageous manifesto, his record of the crimes that *they* had committed against the people who had sailed the beautiful and magnificent glitterships, making the commerce and the wealth of the Seven Worlds possible. They had stolen and ravaged and perverted everything that was glorious.

And when at last he was tired of writing, when he had nothing more to say, he stopped.

Sometimes he masturbated. He thought about the women, the men, the ones who lived beyond mere gender, and the delicious moments he had enjoyed with them. Those were pleasant memories. But most of those people were dead now, the revolution had not been merciful, and his erotic memories were stained by the knowledge of their separate destinies. Occasionally, though, he did think about forcefully pleasuring himself on those he imagined to be his enemies, especially those who had imprisoned him. He did not write about that—just in case any of those might be monitoring his memoirs.

Finally, when he had exhausted himself, he slept. He ate. He exercised. He walked the silent decks. He returned to his cabin and slept again.

And that was his existence.

PART THREE

THE DISPOSED

ONE DAY—IT MIGHT have been a day, it might have been a night, it could have been any intermediate hour—morning, afternoon, dusk, or even that still, small moment before dawn when the darkness at the bottom of the soul rises toward consciousness, but in the emptiness of deep space, the distinctions of time become arbitrary. Any moment can be the moment of despair.

Nevertheless, one day Redmonde was summoned.

He had lost count how many glitterships he'd seen, some of them more than once. Most of them, he didn't even know the name of the vessel. Even that was denied him.

But on this day, he was summoned to a lounge he had never seen before. It was on the counterclockwise wheel, the one previously reserved for the glittership's aristocracy.

By any standards, the lounge was luxurious—not the luxury Redmonde had known in the past, there were no hangings, no tapestries, no silken curtains, no simmering teapots, no goblets, no decanters, no liquors or sweetmeats, no servants, not even a bot—

but still outfitted well enough to present a comfortable and welcoming space, certainly more than the simple surroundings he regularly endured.

Counselor Jezzro sat in a soft chair. He gestured to Redmonde directing him to the seat opposite.

"You're still alive?" Redmonde asked.

"As are you," Jezzro responded. "Now we are both surprised."

"They let you live?"

"I'm still useful. You are not."

"Are you here to pronounce death sentence?"

"Only if you request euthanasia. Do you?"

"No, I do not. As long as I am alive, I am an expense to them. It is a small revenge, but it is all I have. At the moment."

"You expect an opportunity to do more?"

Redmonde shrugged. "I expect nothing."

Jezzro studied the younger man for a moment. "You are still remarkably handsome. A shameful waste of beauty. You still have the soul of a viper."

"Is that why I'm here? So you can insult me?"

"Oh no, I can insult you anywhere. Whether you're present or not. I'm here to inform you of a change in your circumstances."

"A parole."

Jezzro shook his head. "No. Unfortunately for you, there is no mechanism for that. And even if there were, you have no advocates. You are—" Jezzro paused, choosing his next words carefully. "You are regarded as one of the incorrigibles."

"At least I'm good for something. Is that all? No, you said something about a change…"

"Yes. Somewhat. You see, the glitterships have become obsolete. Oh, they will still sail, they are still useful, but—" Jezzro looked pained. "I have to speak carefully. You are not only condemned to an exile from all that you have rejected, the people around you are not allowed discuss anything connected to what you have rejected. It would be regarded as a criminal act. Nevertheless, because other circumstances have changed, your situation has also changed."

Redmonde leaned back in his chair. He folded his arms. Whatever annoyance he might have felt, at least this was a semblance of a conversation. "Tell me," he said. "Take your time. I don't have anything important on my calendar."

Jezzro nodded, not amused. "Portals," he said.

"What's that?"

"Doorways. Tunnels. Holes in space." He pointed to an imaginary place on his left. "Imagine a portal here." He pointed to another imaginary place on his right. "Imagine the other side of that portal over here. Once both sides are in place, you can step into either and step out at the other without passing through the space between."

"Teleportation?"

"No. Not at all. The science is much different. But the effect is the same, instantaneous travel from one place to another. Even from one planet to another. So spaceships become unnecessary."

"Are you telling me that I'm going to go back to—?"

"Don't say it," Jezzro cut him off. "And no, you're not."

"So…what?"

"So," said Counselor Jezzro. "What do we still need ships for?"

Redmonde shrugged. "For the elites? The new elites? The people who will be replacing the people they murdered?"

Jezzro looked sad. He took a breath. "That is the attitude that has defined you as an incorrigible. And no, I will not say anything more about that. I will ask the question again. What do we still need ships for?" He paused. "We have half the portal here. We need a ship to deliver the other half to there. Wherever *there* is."

Redmonde shrugged. "So what? I'm still nowhere, right?"

"Yes, much more nowhere than before," Jezzro said. "This ship you're on. It has a new mission. It's going out. Far out."

"Wait? What?"

Jezzro held up a hand for silence. "This ship will be outfitted with multiple portals. It will deliver them to the outer planets. And then beyond."

"This ship doesn't have the range to—"

"It will. The fuel, the life support systems, even the engines, all of that stays behind, connected to this ship only through the portals it carries. Any ship we build, every ship, will have most of its fuel, engines, and life support systems installed and maintained at the portal source, while only the portal-carrying structures boost. Unlimited access to fuel means unlimited acceleration. Under continuing acceleration, it's projected that this vessel can achieve nearly 90% lightspeed. Halfway to the destination, the ship flips over and begins deceleration. Without the limits of fuel, our only limit now is distance. The possibilities are exciting. Think of it. After we deliver portal systems to Proxima or Sirius or wherever, we can expand from there, pushing through settlements, industries, and more portals to continue the leap outward. Each new world will be a steppingstone to the next and human beings will create a true interstellar network." Visibly excited, Counselor Jezzro had to stop himself, regroup his thoughts. He paused, he raised a single finger as if to illustrate a point. "But...your circumstances, Redmonde, they haven't changed. The glitterships are being refitted. They're all going out. And so are you."

"Wait, what—?"

"The circumstances of your sentence were determined by interplanetary law. You were sentenced to exile from everything you rejected. This is part of it."

Redmonde sagged in his seat.

"Nothing is going to change for you," Jezzro said. "There will be a rotating crew aboard the ship, so you won't be alone. In fact, you will be considered crew. If you wish. All life support, including meals, will be delivered through the portals. So you will have a more varied menu. And in less than a year, maybe a little more, your time, you'll be one of the first human beings to orbit another world. And—when it's finally possible to land on a suitable planet, you can be part of the landing party. There is nothing in your sentence to prohibit that."

"I am comfortable where I am." Redmonde folded his arms in defiance.

"And where you are—where you will be—that is not a circumstance under your control."

"Wait—" Redmonde held up a hand. "What if there's a limit to how far apart the two sides of a portal can be? What if they start failing? I'd be light years from home without food or water or air. It'd be a death sentence."

"There will be some emergency supplies, of course," said Jezzro. "But there's this. There will be multiple portals aboard the ship. If even one of them starts to flicker, everyone on board—including you—will be recalled immediately."

"What if they all collapse at once."

Jezzro shook his head. "Unlikely. There are multiple factors involved in how each portal is maintained, but the math suggests that the reach of portals is unlimited."

"Suggests?"

"Admittedly, we won't know for sure until we know for sure."

"I don't like it."

"You don't have a choice in the matter."

"This could be considered cruel and unusual punishment."

"It's not cruel."

"It's definitely unusual," Redmonde replied.

Jezzro sighed. He rubbed his forehead. When he spoke again, he spoke slowly. "You have not had the opportunity to read The Seven Principles of Organic Government, have you? If you wish, I could provide you with a copy, and associated commentaries."

"Why would I care?"

"It might give you some insight into the circumstances of your sentence. The Seven Principles were the mission statement for the...the shift in authority and the foundation for its Constitution. But I'll give you the short version. Any community, a city, a state, a nation, can be considered a social organism. A healthy organism requires cooperation and contribution from all of its separate organs, and from the cells that make up those organs. Anything that uses resources without a contribution is a cancer on the whole. In a functioning community, participation must be earned or the community has the right to excise the cancer."

"So I'm a cancer on the body—?"

"Technically, yes." Jezzro held up a hand to stop Redmonde from arguing. "Yes, you can argue that there are exceptions, the disabled, the retired, the old and the young, but those exceptions are included in the definitions of contribution. It's in the commentaries. The Principles even make the point that those who have been imprisoned for crimes against the community can still contribute their labor. And that brings us to your situation."

"How so? Am I not already a good example of a bad example?"

"You would be, if anyone knew you were here. Nobody does, except those who are directly responsible for your maintenance." Jezzro sighed. "The single agency that has authority over your maintenance has determined that you will contribute by being a part of this effort. You will be the sole continuing occupant of the outgoing vessel. All the other crews will rotate through the portals. Considering the circumstances of your sentence, you can be allowed a more interactive relationship with them, but the same restrictions will apply. The rotating crews will know that you can have no discussions, no information at all, about anything you have rejected."

Redmonde sat silent, considering Jezzro's words. He unfolded his arms. He rubbed his nose. He scowled. He folded his arms again.

The Counselor continued, "You will be under continuing medical observation to see what effects a person might experience from prolonged exposure to prolonged near-light-speed velocity. Relativity speaking, we expect there will be no effects, but this surveillance will still be a way that you can make a contribution to the social organism."

Redmonde went silent, lost in some deep internal examination. "What if I choose not to contribute? What if I don't accept—"

Jezzro stopped him. He spoke slowly and carefully. "You have no choice in the matter. You took a stand. You were given ample opportunity to recant. You refused. You doubled down. I was there. You were young and foolish, so I advocated mercy. You were judged by the court and you were found guilty, you were sentenced. Now you are older, but you are still foolish. If anything, this is an act of mercy. The alternative has always been execution. This way, you get to be part of a grand adventure."

Now it was Redmonde's turn to speak slowly and carefully. "How many times do I have to say this, Counselor? I have never recognized the authority of this illegal government. I do not recognize its authority now. Whatever so-called punishment anyone seeks to inflict, I consider it illegal. You have control over my body, yes—but you will never have control over my mind."

Jezzro allowed himself a slight smile. "By that very personal standard, any government is illegal to a person who chooses to reject its authority. And people who reject authority tend to reject all authorities, not just governments. Nevertheless, governments exist to provide services that the individuals cannot provide for themselves. Governments have to exist to regulate the channels of commerce for the common good. Regardless of legality, regardless of how a government has come to power, governments exist. This one, at least, operates on a unique principle, I quote, 'This government, of the people, by the people, and for the people, must be accountable *to the people.*'"

"It has not been accountable to me," said Redmonde.

"Why should it? By its standards, you became a criminal when you rejected its authority. But this government has demonstrated its validity by remaining accountable to the majority that authorized it—that majority which regarded you and the people you served as cancers on the economic body. And that does bring me to one final point..."

"There's more?"

Counselor Jezzro cleared his throat. "Only this. In a few days, this ship will be rechristened *The Outward Bound.* It boosts in thirty days, as soon as the portals are installed. The refit will continue even after it boosts. That's another advantage, ships can be maintained, upgraded, remodeled, even in transit. Redmonde, whether you like it or not, you are going to make a contribution to the body politic. You are going to the stars."

Jezzro reached for his cane, began the process of pulling himself to his feet, "And with that, we are done here."

Counselor Jezzro waved to an unseen monitor. Two aides appeared immediately to help him out, leaving Redmonde sitting alone in the lounge.

After a bit, they came to escort him back to his cabin.

Part Four

The Departed

The glittership boosted.

The portal-enhanced engines were small, barely capable of a tenth of a gee, but their thrust was continuous and the increase in velocity was cumulative. Larger engines would be pushed through one of the portals and installed for the much longer journey to Proxima.

The first stop was Ceres in the asteroid belt. A portal station was installed there. After that, the moons of Jupiter. Six portals were stationed. Then Saturn's moons where more portals were delivered. And then out toward Pluto and Sedna.

Redmonde knew little of this. None of the rotating crew had much to say to him. They went about their jobs, either bringing bots and equipment through one of the portals, or ripping out unnecessary equipment and furnishings and sending them back.

It wasn't until *The Outward Bound* was deep into the Oort cloud that a more permanent schedule of rotating crews took over. Six different teams serviced the ship—Red, Blue, Green, Gold, White, and Black.

There were always two teams aboard, serving staggered shifts, fourteen days each. Every seven days, one team rotated out and the next rotated in.

The portals provided food, air, and the occasional visitor, sometimes a team of researchers, occasionally a political figure or a celebrity of some sort. Visiting an outbound ship was a privilege, a perk of celebrity or power. Few of these figures spoke to Redmonde, they had probably been instructed not to.

The one time one of the visitors grew curious enough to draw Redmonde into conversation, the conversation was short. He regarded the visitors as thieves who had displaced the rightful owners of the glittership. His cooperation with any of them varied from reluctance to overt hostility. He kept to his cabin.

All of the cabins in the two rotating wheels had been adjusted to compensate for the thrust of the engines. Eventually, when the glittership was capable of one-gee thrust, the cabins would reorient 90 degrees, and the rotations would be paused.

When the first of the larger engines came through a twelve-meter industrial portal, the bots took twenty days to install and test it. Three small fuel-feeding portals were added and tested, and three days later, the big engine came online, boosting the ship's acceleration to a half gee, creating a genuine sense of gravity in the glittership's main lounge.

Where once the glitterati had convened, hanging from the walls, the floors, the ceilings, to disparage dirtside life, now that space was transformed into multiple useful spaces, a gymnasium where rugged workers exercised between shifts, a cafeteria where they could share their meals and breaks, and even a bath where hot showers could be portaled in and wastewater could be portaled out.

Despite himself, despite his misgivings, Redmonde was curious enough to investigate all the changes in the glittership.

One afternoon, by his clock, he came down to the former lounge to see what changes the crews had made. He looked around the space, now stripped of its extravagance and newly equipped for rest and recreation, and found himself reluctantly approving. Perhaps he'd been living the life of an ascetic for too long.

He wasn't planning to be a frequent visitor to this space, he had learned to live without much human interaction, but several of the crew welcomed him and invited him to join them at their table. He didn't intend to be friendly, but he found he enjoyed the occasional game of dominoes and their other exercises in amateur entertainment. They weren't bad musicians, and they had a lot of fun learning new pieces. Dershem the trumpeter explained, "The ship runs itself. So we have a lot of time to play. The music is another world."

One afternoon, Redmonde accidentally revealed he still had some skill at demonstrative dance. The presence of simulated gravity made some of the steps easier, but others that required one gee had to be adjusted. Afterward, their scattered applause embarrassed him. He hadn't experienced the approval of other human beings in years.

They didn't talk politics and they didn't speak of his exile, so he didn't either. They talked about music, jazz and classical and rock, and they mostly got along.

Redmonde stopped taking his meals alone, he joined the others in the refitted lounge. When he had nothing to say, which was often, he listened with interest to their discussions of ship maintenance and portal systems. Sometimes he asked questions, sometimes they answered.

The glittership was accelerating and the teams were noticing the time-dilation effect. They reported they were missing two extra days back home. It wasn't exactly a complaint, just another part of the adventure, but some of them wondered if their service aboard might be some kind of biological experiment, because bots did most of the real work.

Like the teams, the bots also rotated out for service and maintenance. There were few jobs aboard that required human supervision. Redmonde's input was limited to suggestions about the music or other entertainments.

Some of the team members tolerated him, a few ignored him, several were genuinely friendly, they'd never met a real criminal before, and after a bit, they all regarded him as the grand old man of the glittership, a kind of honorary host.

Redmonde tolerated some, appreciated a few, liked only a couple. He was close to none. And yet... there were moments.

Lara had dark hair that shimmered with crimson-amber highlights, an attractive contrast to her dusky skin, she was a trainee on the Blue Team—and she was fascinated by Redmonde, a living remnant of a lost but fabled past.

After the evening meal, after the music ended, she sat with him in the lounge, sharing coffee and cakes sent up from someplace that nobody talked about. When she felt the moment was right, when she felt he might be willing to answer, she asked him questions about the fabled past, always carefully phrased.

Redmonde mostly shook his head. He didn't want to revisit those times. He had slowly come to the realization that in his exile aboard *The Outward Bound*, he was still freer than he had ever been while enslaved to Lady Daltimore's service.

But Lara persisted. "I think your story needs to be told."

"Another condemnation of the perverse glories of the past?"

"No," said Lara. "That's just propaganda. I want to know about the people, who they really were, how they lived and thought. What were they like?"

"The current theory," said Redmonde, "is that excessive wealth and power are dissociative influences. They will corrupt even the most noble. Did I get that right?"

"I think human beings are more complicated than that," Lara replied. "Can we talk about you?"

Redmonde sighed. "I was transferred from one glittership to another, until I was assigned permanent residence here. What more do you need to know?"

"You saw all the glitterships?"

"Most of them."

"What were they like?"

He shrugged. "Lavish, if you were a passenger. Perhaps not for the crews—they surrendered immediately. So maybe they had feelings of resentment. I probably shouldn't talk about that. I have been told that my opinions are unpopular. And I'm tired of the arguments. Nobody wins. Nobody even listens."

"You can say what you want," said Lara. "We are very far away from everything."

"No, we're not. I know this much. The portals have destroyed the concept of distance. Even the relativistic effects of near-light-speed acceleration are mostly sidestepped."

"Slightly, yes. Not completely. That's why they rotate the crews. Fourteen days here is twenty back there."

"Whatever." He waved it away. "I'm not going to violate my...I guess you could call it a parole. That might put you in danger. An authority that would do this to me, I don't know what they might do to you if you encouraged me to break the law."

"I appreciate your concern," said Lara. She smiled gently. "They did tell us to be careful around you. They said you had no feelings for others. But maybe they were wrong about that. I think you have strong feelings."

Redmonde shrugged. "I haven't had any feelings in a long time. I poured them into my writing until I had nothing left to say. Now I just survive. I sleep, I wake, I eat, I defecate. My days are all the same. But I endure. Any resentment I might have for...for my circumstances, no crewperson should be the target of it"

"You've given this a lot of thought."

"I've had a lot of time."

"But you've had no real companionship...?"

"I've had music. I've had entertainments. I've had solitary games. And I've had access to a sex-bot. I will acknowledge that my life onboard has not been entirely unpleasant. I am not being abused, just removed and disconnected from...from the things I rejected. It's supposed to be punishment, I guess, but...the disassociation from all the things I learned to hate, maybe that's no punishment at all."

Lara hesitated. "Perhaps I shouldn't ask this, but I will. Have you changed your mind at all? About... your situation?"

Redmonde considered the question for a long time before answering. "It doesn't matter, does it? I'm here. I can't be anywhere else."

"You said...all the things you learned to hate...?"

"Do you really want to know?"

She nodded.

"I have reason to hate. A lot of reasons. I was abandoned. I grew up in a crèche. I was bullied and abused by the bigger inmates because I was smaller and smarter and prettier. Yes, prettier. I was surrounded by pain and ugliness. There was no safety anywhere. But eventually I discovered I could hide from the worst of it inside the music rooms. Music felt like an escape, it took me away to places where others couldn't touch me. It was the music that saved me. I found a keyboard and I learned I could make music, whatever I wanted to hear.

"I was good at it, good enough to attract the attention of a patron—a patron who wanted a useful and affectionate bedmate. I learned fast. I had to. The alternative would have been a return to ugliness.

"I went through several patrons, some of them treated me well. I liked being at their tables. If you've never had plantation-grown food, you've never known real food. It was good. And they provided access to education and entertainment and exercises I had never known were possible. I cherished the service. Eventually, they thought I would benefit from access to the kind of exalted education that would make me a suitable companion for any of the glitterati—and when I finally demonstrated some excellence at certain skills of companionship, they sold me to Lady Daltimore. Should I resent them for that? Or should I thank them? They made it possible for me to have a better life than anything I could have imagined or achieved without them. So yes, I hate the circumstances that I escaped, and I enjoyed the life I had for too brief a while, and I hate the people who took it away from me. And their pathetic justifications as well. It's all noise in service of power. Am I wrong? Am I wrong to feel this way?"

Lara put her hand on his. "I am not your judge," she said. "May I ask you this? Did Lady Daltimore appreciate your...your services?"

"She kept me as her favorite. Does that answer your question?"

"And you have had no other since then?"

"The sex-bot tells me that I'm enthusiastic."

"Was that a joke?"

"You'd have to ask the sex-bot."

Lara pulled her hand back. "I think, maybe, we should stop here. If that's all right with you."

"As you wish," Redmonde nodded. "I am at your service."

"Is that how you responded to Lady Daltimore?"

"It is how I was trained," he said. He rose then, heading back to his cabin, leaving Lara to her thoughts.

The conversation troubled Redmonde. Her hand on his was a memory both pleasant and disturbing.

A few shifts later, the Blue Team reported that *The Outward Bound* was now accelerating away from the Sol system fast enough to achieve a two-for-one time-dilation effect. A month would pass on the home planet for every fourteen days the team spent onboard the glittership.

Redmonde sought out Lara in the lounge. She smiled when she saw him. He sat down opposite her and pointed to the stripes on her sleeve. "You've been promoted."

She dismissed the thought. "It's a service thing, based on days spent here. But I am being paid at the home days rate, so it feels like a raise. If inflation doesn't wipe it out. Economics, ugh." She made a face.

"Money is another tool of oppression—" he started to say, then stopped himself. "Never mind. Sorry."

She nodded. "I'm familiar with the theory." She reached over and took his hand. "The last of the big engines has been assembled, it should be coming through the portal while the Blue Team is still on board. Once that engine is installed and brought online, *The Outward Bound* could boost at full gee. Maybe even a smidge more. Whatever they decide, you should expect to arrive at Proxima in less than a year. The rest of us, portaling back and forth between home and here, this journey is a five-year commitment for us. Once we deliver the ship, the research teams come aboard. They're really getting eager. I should warn you, some of them will be visiting soon. More when you get closer to Proxima. They don't need to, there are training mockups back on—there are simulators for them to train on. But they want to see the real ship."

Redmonde said, "Uh-huh. I've been accessing the daily status reports. They're not coming through as fast as they used to. Time-dilation. You have a family, don't you?"

Lara blinked, surprised. "I didn't think you were interested."

"I'm not. I was trying to be polite. I've been reading about social skills. Manners."

"Ah," said Lara. "You almost made it, but admitting you're not interested nullified the question."

"You're not a glitterati. The transactions are very different. You don't ask an elite personal questions. But you can ask an associate, because that can be necessary information."

"So I'm an associate?" She let go of his hand.

"I'm not sure what the relationship is," he said. "You're not my jailer. You're not an associate. You're not really a colleague, are you? And I don't think we're friends, are we? At best, we are acquaintances engaged in a common effort."

She leaned back in her chair, studying him. "You really are precise in your language, aren't you?"

"It's how I was trained. The elites don't waste time. They require accuracy."

Lara considered the assertion. "You are a very complex man," she said.

"Yes," he agreed. "That is accurate."

She decided to change the subject. "My family misses me. Every homecoming is a little longer than before, so we have a party to catch me up on the news. But really, I think they're mostly trying to maintain the emotional connection. I keep telling them they don't have to worry, but my family is old-fashioned. They're from—sorry."

"I've never had a family," Redmonde said.

"Not even a family of friends or associates or...? No one you're close to?"

He shook his head.

She fell silent. She didn't know what to say to that.

"We were taught that associations are risky. Trust is the first step to betrayal."

"There's no room for love in that philosophy."

"Love is a feeling. Feelings are like farts. They evaporate."

Lara realized something then. "That's what they taught you. Isn't it? Slogans. Not facts, not experiences. Just something to say instead of your feelings."

"I have feelings," he said. "But feelings do not have me."

"That's another soundbite."

He didn't answer.

"I read what you wrote," she said. "Some of it. It was made available to us, so we could understand you better. I've been trying to reconcile that with the man you are, the one sitting across from me."

"I was sick," he said. "I forgot myself. I forgot to be the person I was supposed to be. My emotions took over for a while, so I wrote those things to complete my anger and get those feelings out of my body. I mostly succeeded."

"Yes, apparently you did."

"That was an insult, wasn't it?"

"You're not stupid. Yes, it was."

"Then this conversation is over." He rose stiffly and returned to his cabin—only realizing once he was there that he had acted out of anger. And the subsequent self-annoyance he felt was another emotion as well.

"I have been around these people too much," he said aloud. He made an appointment with the sex-bot. Maybe that would help. If nothing else, it would be a physical release.

PART FIVE

THE DESTINATION

PROXIMA CENTAURI IS a red dwarf, known to have six planets, three of which were detected by Earth-based telescopes and three more that were later determined by analysis of long-term variations in the observable bodies. The math implied other planets as well.

Proxima B orbits in Proxima Centauri's habitable zone, the range where temperatures are right for liquid water to exist on its surface. But Proxima Centauri is a red dwarf and a flare star, it's also expected to have very high ultra-violet radiation, so the planet's habitability is highly uncertain. But it was also the closest, a good first test of an interstellar portal.

After the final engine was brought online, after the glittership achieved one-gee acceleration, the advance teams started coming aboard in shifts. First they needed to deliver and assemble the equipment they would need when *The Outward Bound* arrived on station. Then they would refit the ship for the assembly of landing probes to drop portals on the surface. Eventually, they would assemble the machines that created portals. They'd bring through more bots, more drones, more ships.

Halfway there, *The Outward Bound* stopped accelerating. She coasted at 83% light-speed for several days while her crews prepared her for flipover and deceleration. It was a period of celebration and anticipation and uncertainty. There was too much at stake. All non-essential personnel were sent back through the portals until the engines were brought back online and full deceleration was established.

Redmonde floated in the lounge, enjoying the liberation from what passed for gravity on the glittership. He had no duties, he wasn't even an official observer. There had been some discussion about evacuating him with the others, but as there was no place for him on the other side, that conversation died in committee.

But flipover was accomplished without incident and the engines came back online as expected. The maneuver was so routine it was boring. The glittership had to burn off a lot of speed. The time-dilation effect put the onboard crews away from home for several months. But it also gave them several months respite before returning for their next shift. But it wouldn't be a vacation. After debriefing, they would have additional training for the next part of the mission.

When the Blue Team came back, Redmonde did not seek out Lara.

His last conversation with her had been uncomfortable. He was well aware of his emotional reactions, but that was not the primary reason. He had made up his mind not to allow any more contact with her. She was deliberately trying to create emotional reactions. He wouldn't allow that. Detachment was survival. Connection was unnecessary. And painful.

So she came to his cabin.

"May I come in?"

"I would prefer that you didn't."

"I want to apologize."

"There's no need. You can go."

"I'm not stupid, Redmonde. I know you're avoiding me."

"I'm not stupid either. Go away."

"I can't."

"Yes, you can."

"No, I can't. It's part of my duties to report on your mental health."

"I'm fine. There, you're done. Now, go away."

"Please open the door."

"No."

"I'm not going away until I see you."

"Why didn't you tell me you were monitoring me."

"I've seen you pretend to be sane. You're not very good at it."

"Neither are you."

"I don't have to be."

"Then we're even."

"Okay, fine. Now open your door."

Silence. For a moment.

He opened the door and looked at her. "It's been awhile," he said.

"Longer for me than for you, but yes. May I come in?"

"There's no place to sit."

"Then let's go to the lounge."

"You asked to come in."

"Okay, fine."

She sat at the desk and swiveled around to face him, sitting on the bed. "How are you doing? What are you feeling? Are you okay?"

"I'm fine. I'm good. I'm as calm as anyone could be under these circumstances. There, we're done. You can go now."

She sighed. "You're really a jerk, aren't you? Is that authentic enough?"

"Is that what you said about me in your report? All your reports?"

"Not exactly, no. I said your social skills were underdeveloped. But it means the same thing."

"Has anything changed?" Redmonde asked. He answered his own question. "No, I don't think so. Therefore, there's no reason for me to change. If the people you represent wanted to see a different me, they'd put me in a different circumstance. That they have not is evidence that they do not want me to change. So really, the only thing you need to report is that I'm coping as well as can be expected, considering, etc. Blah, blah, blah."

"You know? You're right." She made as if to rise, then sat back again. "You're my only patient right now. In the past, I've worked with all kinds of people— and despite any judgments I might have had at the beginning, I usually fell in love with all my clients. No, not romantic love, I know you're unfamiliar with all the different iterations of the word, but I did love my clients because of what they brought to the process. They brought a commitment. They wanted to be more aware, more effective, more productive. They wanted to be healthier. But you, Redmonde—" She shook her head. "You're stuck. You have no commitment, do you?"

"Commitment to what?" he asked blankly.

"Anything," she replied.

"Why?" he asked. "Look around. This is it. This is my world. This is my life. This is me. There's no opportunity for advancement in this career. So...what can I commit to?"

"So far, the only thing you seem to be committed to is staying stuck in the same place."

"This place is traveling at 83% of the speed of

light. Well, it was. We're decelerating now. I don't think that qualifies as stuck."

"Don't play word games, you know what I mean."

"Lara, you are wasting your time here. I would say you are wasting my time, but time is all I have. You, at least, are a pleasant enough diversion. Yes, you're right, I am a jerk—and I have no reason to change. Other human beings taught me that there is no value in trust or affection. I have never had reason to learn any of those things that you and your colleagues seem to value, compassion, empathy, connection, trust—all of that."

"I guess I was wrong," she said. "I had thought that perhaps you and I—"

"Yes, I considered it too. But it was obvious from the beginning that you had an agenda. Everybody has an agenda. It's hardwired into the species. Your agenda did not match mine. I humored you because it amused me to do so, because it was a way to pass the time. But I see no reason to continue. If you want to keep monitoring my mental health, you can, but nothing's going to change. There might be more to life than this, but I will never know it, will I?"

Lara nodded. She stood up. She went to the door. She looked back to Redmonde. "I will say this. Your commitment is impressive."

"Yes, you can put that in your report."

"I will," she said. The door slid shut behind her.

He never saw her again.

After that, he spent less and less time with each returning crew. They bored him. And perhaps the feeling was mutual. He had nothing new to offer them and they were forbidden to give him any news of the Seven Worlds. So he retreated to his cabin, to his books, his music, and the occasional in-and-out with the sex-bot.

He maintained. He endured. He inhaled, exhaled, ate, slept, defecated, urinated, exercised, masturbated, listened to music, watched what he was allowed to watch on his cabin screen, and occasionally sat down and wrote something that no one would ever read.

Time passed, slowly on *The Outward Bound*, but still much faster on the worlds he no longer remembered.

The glittership decelerated.

Only a few weeks of shipboard time.

And eventually it approached Proxima Centauri. The pilot crew came aboard and adjusted its course to slingshot around the star, where they would make close observations of its behavior. The glittership would head outward to catch up with Proxima B, match its orbit, and eventually settle into a polar circuit around the planet for detailed mapping of its surface. After a few weeks of that, the first landing site would be selected and the first portal would be dropped.

Despite his deliberate detachment from the others, Redmonde still followed every part of the process, the approach to Proxima Centauri, the adjustment of the glittership's course, the close study of the red star as they swung around it, the long approach to Proxima B, and all the separate course adjustments to put the ship into a polar orbit, and finally the studies of the planet's surface, it's continents and seas, the deserts at its equator, and the icecaps at its poles. The planet had its own naked beauty.

Exploratory drones were dropped to the surface, sending back views of vast empty landscapes, roiling seas racked by violent winds, vistas of rugged mountains and unapproachable terrain, and even hints of primitive life forms scrabbling for existence wherever they could.

Redmonde sat in the galley and listened to the exploration crews arguing about terraforming, whether it was possible, how to do it, and if human beings could adapt to 1.34 gravity. The long-term health issues would be severe, perhaps only rotating crews would serve downside, it might be better to establish stations on either of the planet's two moons, the conversations continued endlessly.

Because portals were always open, both ends had to be triple-contained before either end was opened. The engineering was methodical and exact. It had to be. Portals were only opened again when they were enclosed in stormproof, quakeproof, triple airlock structures, often underground with meters of shielding on all sides. Even the smallest differences in atmospheric pressure would create an unstoppable wind. Portals could be closed, but once a portal was shut down, it couldn't be reopened.

The portal ship landed safely to great cheers from the monitoring crew. Bottles of champagne were opened. Redmonde snagged a glass from a passing tray. Nobody objected.

The next step would be to unseal the glittership side of the portal in an airlocked chamber. The landing drone would unseal its portal, and the airlocked chamber would fill with the local atmosphere, it would be measured, tested, examined, scrutinized, and scanned. That would take days, maybe even weeks, before the landing crew could go down. First, they would send all the drones and vehicles they would need for local exploration. Then, finally, the landing team would suit up and step through for onsite inspection. When they were satisfied they had found a suitable site, they would transport the portal and the machinery to construct a secure enclosure would be sent down.

The hours turned into days, days of careful planning turned into weeks of preparation. Specific tools and equipment came through portals that opened to places 4.33 light-years away. Much of the planning and provision was on the faraway side. Every step of every procedure was reviewed and tested and reviewed again before approval came through.

There were adjustments to be made. Proxima B

was rugged and unruly, but there were no serious missteps, no catastrophes. Decades of thought had gone into each of these moments.

Step by step, Redmonde followed all the procedures closely. A promise had been made to him, he intended to have it kept. Something Counselor Jezzro had said, before *The Outward Bound* was launched, "... when it's finally possible to land on a suitable planet, you can be part of the landing party. There is nothing in your sentence to prohibit that."

So when the sealed enclosure was up and running. When the portal tracks were connected and the portal trains were arriving on Proxima B, Redmonde went to the SOPE, the Senior Onsite Portal Engineer to remind her of Jezzro's promise.

Nyota Mmbele was a small woman, dark-skinned, with hair tied close to her head, always carrying a tablet, sometimes two. She was aware of Redmonde's situation, she had exchanged polite words with him, answering his occasional questions, but little more. Now, she listened politely to his request. "I want to go down."

She responded with a slight frown. "There's nothing in my instructions about that. I'll have to ask the agency administrators. I'll get back to you." She walked away and began dictating a note to one of her tablets.

Redmonde wasn't surprised. Lady Daltimore would have turned to an associate and said, "Make it happen," and that would have been all that was necessary. Bureaucracies were just another way to say no. But there was no reason to deny his request. He was banned only from...those worlds they didn't mention around him. He wasn't banned from any other world.

Two shifts later, Mmbele summoned him to her office. "I'm sorry," she said. "Your request has been denied."

"Huh? Why?"

"I've been informed that Proxima B is now legally a colony."

"But it's not one of the...you know."

"No, it is not." She did not look happy. "But, as I have been made to understand, the terms of your sentence cannot be argued. You are prohibited from setting foot on any world that shares jurisdiction. I have no authority to let you leave this ship."

Redmonde sagged. "I don't believe this," he said. "This isn't right." He took a breath. "But I should have expected it. There is no mercy here. It's not your fault. You're just another servant of their authority— whoever they are now." A thought occurred to him. "What if I escaped?"

"That's not possible."

"But what if I did?"

"You wouldn't be allowed to return," she said. She picked up her tablet then and read from it. "I am required to inform you that you are hereby prohibited from accessing any of the portals for any reason, with the singular exception of the mandatory evacuation of this vessel in the event of a life-threatening emergency." She interrupted herself to annotate, "Please don't try anything. There are safeguards."

She looked back to her tablet and continued. "This restriction will include every destination that the agency intends to explore and install portals on. Therefore, you are preemptively forbidden to leave this ship, unless you are specifically transferred to another."

Mmbele lowered the tablet and looked at Redmonde directly. "They made it very clear, and I have no intention of defying their instructions. You are not to be allowed access to any location under the agency's jurisdiction, and that must include every planet, moon, or asteroid that this ship might visit in the future." She added, "Unless there's a revolution and a new government establishes control of the agency and changes the law, but at the moment, that's unlikely."

"Of course. Tyrants always protect their tyrannies."

"Thank you for that insight, Mr. Redmonde," Mmbele stood up. "I believe we're through. We're having prime rib tonight. I'll have your dinner delivered to your cabin."

"Faux rib. Grown in a tank. Not real food."

"It's a courtesy. If you prefer something else—"

"It's protein. Injected, fortified, enhanced protein."

He shrugged. "Bring it. I have to eat."

"Thank you. You may leave now."

Redmonde returned to his cabin and stayed there for three weeks. He came out only to exercise in the gym, that was his one concession to circumstances, his only acknowledgment that there were others on whom he depended.

And then, one afternoon, or evening, or morning, or whenever, Redmonde went to the galley, where the entire Red Crew was sharing their last big meal with the Blue Crew before the Green Team shifted in.

He strode in angrily, spewing and shouting. "Injustice! Tyranny! Enablers! All of you! I'm enduring a permanent exile! And you, all of you—jailers! Tormentors! No conscience! No integrity! Nothing! Slaves and slaveholders! Not a gram of honor in the whole ugly lot of you! Pigs content with the swill of tyrants!"

Perhaps they were ready for this. Perhaps that was a permanent part of their duty aboard. Whatever, there were men who grabbed him and sedated him and secured him in his cabin.

He was not allowed out for three shifts, only under supervision, and only after his medications were adjusted.

Eventually, because he had nothing else to do, Redmonde reexamined the circumstances of his outburst. He didn't regret what he'd said. The words were true enough. He only regretted that he had succumbed to his simmering anger, that he had allowed others to see him as an out-of-control emotional being.

After a while, he did understand—his anger was justified. It was still justified. These circumstances weren't just unfair, they were vindictive. Under any rational system of law, he would have been eligible for parole after a predetermined time. Here, there was no possibility of parole. His sentence was cruel.

But if he gave in to anger, he would be giving them the victory. They wanted to see him hurting. That was the goal of punishment, the anguish of the target, the victim. Therefore, he would not give them that victory. Never again.

Resignation to his fate? No. Quiet, stubborn, resistance. Cooperation only for survival—for as long as he survived, as long as they had to see what they were doing to him, he would be punishing them with the ugly evidence of their cruelty.

He reinvented his resolve. And every day that passed became a further victory in his silent campaign of resistance. He returned to his routines, meals, lounge, gymnasium, sex-bot. He spoke to no one unless spoken to. He answered only the most specific questions, otherwise he remained silent.

In his cabin, he occasionally ranted, long ugly screeds of rage—not because he needed to vent as much as he needed to clear his mind of the detritus of emotion. Afterward, he was empty and calm again.

He knew they were monitoring him, so he tailored his rants appropriately.

He had no visitors until the newly appointed Gold Team leader knocked on his door. The intrusion annoyed him. They were supposed to leave him alone. That was the policy. He opened the door resentfully. "What?"

A woman he didn't recognize stood there. She wore a Gold Team uniform. She carried a tablet. She looked official. He waited for her to speak.

"The colony teams have left the ship. They didn't think you wanted to be disturbed, so they asked me to say goodbye for them. The orbital station and the planet-side stations are all functioning, so *The Outward Bound* is no longer needed here. I'm sorry, we've never met. I'm Ander-Jane Huang and I'll be captaining the next part of the mission. We're breaking orbit in three days, for Ross128. I thought you should know. Also, the itinerary for this ship's next seven destinations has been posted. If you're interested."

She added, "Personally, I have no feelings one way or the other about you. I have been given no instructions except to provide you with the necessities of life. For my part, that will include access to the lounge, the gym, the entertainment section, the sex-bots, and any other parts of the ship open to nonessential personnel. You will be considered a passenger and you will be treated as one. You may take your meals in the galley or the lounge, but as you have already established, you are not to engage with any member of the crew at any time or in any way. You will respect these conditions or you will be restricted to your cabin, is that clear? Don't speak. Just nod your head."

He nodded.

"Thank you. If you have any questions, refer them to one of my assistants. I intend no further contact with you. Nod your head."

"Thank you. We're done." She turned and left.

"Nicely done," said Redmonde, his equivalent of a respectful compliment. He closed the door and returned to his solitude.

Behind him, nothing. In front of him, more solitude.

He thought about resistance.

There weren't many ways he could.

But, he wasn't stupid.

He could also imagine the consequences.

PART SIX

THE DISPOSITION

LIKE THE PUFF of a dandelion, the starships flew out, not just from the home system, but from every new portal that was opened. They leapt from star to star, and each new station was a launch pad for the next exploration.

In less than five decades, ships went to Barnard's Star and Sirius, Procyon and Tau Ceti, Gliese 667Cc, Aldebaran, 61 Cygni, Groombridge, Arcturus, Capella, and Vega. Achernar, Ursa Major, and beyond. Not every system was amenable to life, but every system was something to study, and every system was a steppingstone to the next.

They weren't all glitterships. Most were just portal containers, but the converted glitterships remained the pride of the fleet. *The Outward Bound* headed toward Rigel and someday perhaps, future crews would take her out toward Betelgeuse and Polaris.

She'd been updated, refitted, strengthened, converted, even expanded until she was no longer just a glittership but an assembly of pods and containers and warehouses and giant engines to push them to near lightspeed. She was famous as the farthest ship.

And wherever she went, wherever any of the ships went, so did the portals. Portals could be pushed through other portals, so in short time, the network looked like a giant, spherical spiderweb, with every station connected to every other station. No one was ever more than three stations away from anywhere they wanted to go.

And that was when Redmonde made his escape.

The details are irrelevant, they have been dramatized in multiple ways—books, music, plays, movies, and mini-series—and sometimes even accurately.

Redmonde's escape exposed several vulnerabilities in the portal network, all of which were subsequently addressed. And his eventual fate did serve as a warning to others.

It began with a change in government, not a revolution, but a shift in context. With the human race expanding to the stars, with the inevitable time-dilation effects of leaping across vast distances, with the advancement of cultural imperatives, the ideological transformation was inevitable.

Every star system represented a unique set of circumstances, a challenge to the ingenuity of those who chose to live there. Therefore every star system required its own local authority. But…every connected star system would also have to recognize the higher authority of the Universal Compact to function as a member of the network. Most did. It was to their benefit.

With that expansion came a reorganization of the Charter. Laws had to be adjusted to cover the expanded circumstances of human exploration. And somewhere in there, one of the almost overlooked details evaluated by an intelligence engine, the circumstances of Redmonde's exile were reexamined. He was still forbidden to stand on the surface of any world—those were still under the umbrella of the expanded Compact, but there was nothing in the original sentence that prohibited him from traveling across the interstellar portal network, from any space habitat to any other.

And that was all Redmonde needed.

In a very short time, he flashed across the network, stepping from one portal to the next as quickly as he could cross the concourse. Somewhere in there, he invented a new identity, became someone else, became another, and a third, but he never set foot dirtside. If and when they ever caught up with him, they would not be able to charge him with violating the terms of his exile.

And that should have been the end of it.

In some of the dramatizations, Redmonde has

been portrayed as a ghost, a legend, a *Flying Dutchman*, condemned to an immortal existence among the stars, traveling from portal to portal, trapped in his own tragic destiny.

But no.

Redmonde wanted to demonstrate that he was a free man in a network of restrictions. So he flashed from portal to portal, his goal to demonstrate that there was nowhere in the network he could not go.

———————

There is a monument to Redmonde circling Luna. It can be seen by telescope. It is also Redmonde's tomb.

Portal exits are sealed in a triple shell, never unsealed until they are installed in a securely sealed triple-airlocked enclosure. Portal exits are manufactured and shipped outward. Many wait in orbit around Luna.

Redmonde, unwisely, stepped into one of those sealed portals and was instantly flattened, crushed to oblivion. The internal width of a portal containment is less than a fifth of a meter.

Redmonde's path had been tracked, but not restricted. When the portal authority ultimately discovered how Redmonde had died, decisions were made—too late to help him, but finally a singular contribution to others.

The portal containers were widened, and even

secured with life support and communication systems in case anyone else might make the same mistake.

But Redmonde's final leap will remain his final exile.

It will circle Luna for another five billion years—until Sol exhausts the hydrogen at its core and expands into a red giant, devouring its innermost planets.

But by then, if there is still a human species, or whatever it may have evolved into, it will be very far away.

Meanwhile, in the here and now, in the realm of stories and dreams, Redmonde is still out there, still flashing from portal to portal, and still searching for a place called peace.

ABOUT THE AUTHOR

David Gerrold's work is known around the world. His novels and stories have been translated into more than a dozen languages. His TV scripts are estimated to have been seen by more than a billion viewers.

Gerrold's prolific output includes stage shows, teleplays, film scripts, educational films, computer software, comic books, more than 50 novels and anthologies, and hundreds of articles, columns, and short stories.

He has worked on a dozen different TV series, including *Star Trek, Land of the Lost, Twilight Zone, Star Trek: The Next Generation, Babylon 5,* and *Sliders.* He is the author of *Star Trek*'s most popular episode "The Trouble With Tribbles."

Many of his novels are classics of the science fiction genre, including *The Man Who Folded Himself,* the ultimate time travel story, and *When HARLIE Was One,* considered one of the most thoughtful tales of artificial intelligence ever written. His stunning novels on ecological invasion, *A Matter For Men, A Day For Damnation, A Rage For Revenge,* and *A Season For Slaughter,* have all been best sellers with a devoted fan following. His young adult series, *The Dingilliad,* traces the healing journey of a troubled family from Earth to a far-flung colony on another world. His *Star Wolf* series of novels about the psychological nature of interstellar war are in development as a television series.

A ten-time Hugo and Nebula award nominee, David Gerrold is also a recipient of the Skylark Award for Excellence in Imaginative Fiction, the Bram Stoker Award for Superior Achievement in Horror, and the Forrest J. Ackerman lifetime achievement award.

In 1995, Gerrold shared the adventure of how he adopted his son in *The Martian Child,* a semi-autobiographical tale of a science fiction writer who adopts a little boy, only to discover he might be a Martian. *The Martian Child* won the science fiction triple crown: the Hugo, the Nebula, and the Locus. It was the basis for the 2007 film *Martian Child* starring John Cusack and Amanda Peet.

Gerrold's greatest writing strengths are generally acknowledged to be his readable prose, his easy wit, his facility with action, the accuracy of his science, and the passions of his characters. An accomplished lecturer and world traveler, he has made appearances all over the United States, England, Europe, Canada, Australia, and New Zealand. His easy-going manner and disarming humor have made him a perennial favorite with audiences.

David Gerrold is the 2022 winner of the Robert A. Heinlein Award.